Caring
Eggs and Babies

Written by Brylee Gibson

Rigby

This mother has babies.
They are in a den.
The mother will care
for the babies.

den

This mother has babies.
The babies are
on the mother's back.
The mother will care
for the babies.

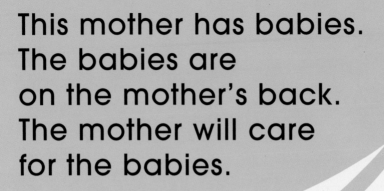

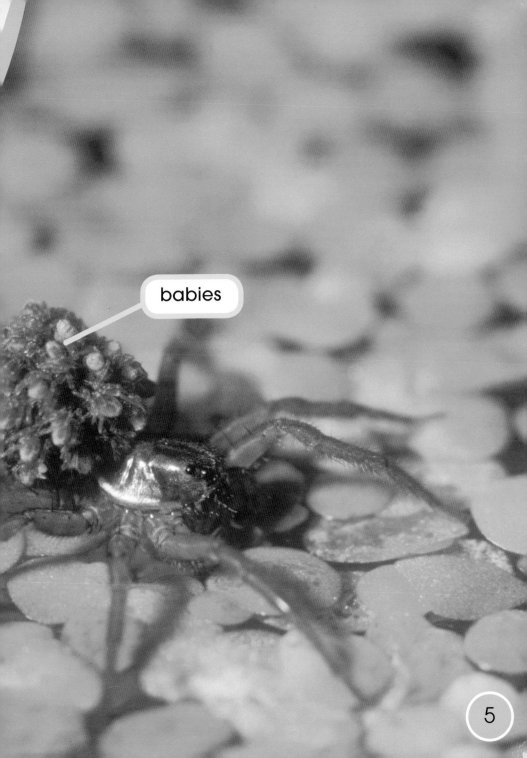

babies

This father has babies.
They are in his pouch.
The father will care
for the babies.

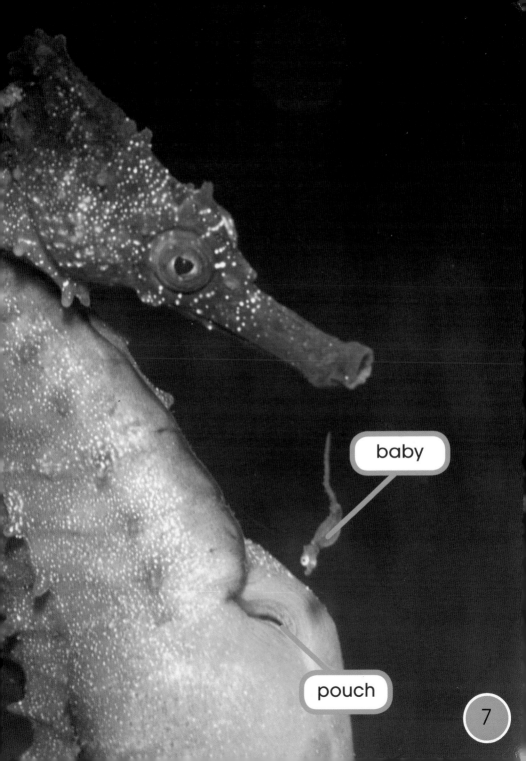

baby

pouch

This father has eggs.
They are on his legs.
The father will care
for the eggs.

eggs

This father has eggs.
They are in the nest.
The father will care
for the eggs.

eggs

Look at the babies.
This mother **and** father
will care for the babies.

Index

Guide Notes

Title: Caring for Eggs and Babies
Stage: Early (2) – Yellow

Genre: Nonfiction
Approach: Guided Reading
Processes: Thinking Critically, Exploring Language, Processing Information
Written and Visual Focus: Photographs (static images), Index, Labels
Word Count: 95

THINKING CRITICALLY
(sample questions)
- Look at the title and read it to the children.
- Ask the children what they know about animals that take care of eggs or babies. Discuss with the children how sometimes one or both parents take care of the eggs or the babies.
- Focus the children's attention on the index. Ask: "What are you going to find out about in this book?"
- If you want to find out about fathers with babies, which pages would you look on?
- If you want to find out about fathers with eggs, which pages would you look on?
- If you want to find out about mothers with babies, which pages would you look on?
- Look at pages 2 and 3, and 6 and 7. What is different about the way these animals care for their babies?
- Why do you think the spider on pages 4 and 5 might carry her babies on her back?

EXPLORING LANGUAGE

Terminology
Title, cover, photographs, author, photographers

Vocabulary
Interest words: care, babies, eggs, den, pouch, back
High-frequency word: his
Positional words: in, on

Print Conventions
Capital letter for sentence beginnings, periods